Hauntings

DiscoverRoo
An Imprint of Pop!
popbooksonline.com

HAUNTED JEWELS

by Elizabeth Andrews

abdobooks.com

Published by Pop!, a division of ABDO, PO Box 398166, Minneapolis, Minnesota 55439. Copyright © 2022 by Abdo Consulting Group, Inc. International copyrights reserved in all countries. No part of this book may be reproduced in any form without written permission from the publisher. DiscoverRoo™ is a trademark and logo of Pop!.

Printed in the United States of America, North Mankato, Minnesota.

102021
012022

THIS BOOK CONTAINS RECYCLED MATERIALS

Cover Photos: Everett Collection Historical/Alamy Stock Photo; Shutterstock Images, (pattern)

Interior Photos: Shutterstock Images, 1, 5, 21, 23, 26; Royal Court of Sweden/Wikimedia, 6; Glasshouse Images/Shutterstock, 7; Smithsonian Institution Archives/Wikimedia, 8; Archives du 7e Art/20th Century Fox, 9; Tom Kelley Archive/Getty Images, 13; Bettmann/Getty Images, 14; AFP/Staff/Getty Images, 17; Peter J. Yost/Wikimedia, 29

Editor: Tyler Gieseke
Series Designer: Laura Graphenteen

Library of Congress Control Number: 2021943410
Publisher's Cataloging-in-Publication Data
Names: Andrews, Elizabeth, author.
Title: Haunted jewels / by Elizabeth Andrews
Description: Minneapolis, Minnesota : Pop!, 2022 | Series: Hauntings | Includes online resources and index
Identifiers: ISBN 9781098241247 (lib. bdg.) | ISBN 9781644946770 (pbk.) | ISBN 9781098241940 (ebook)
Subjects: LCSH: Jewelry--Juvenile literature. | Ghosts--Juvenile literature. | Spirits--Juvenile literature. | Ghost Stories--Juvenile literature.
Classification: DDC 133.1--dc23

Pop open this book and you'll find QR codes loaded with information, so you can learn even more!

Scan this code* and others like it while you read, or visit the website below to make this book pop!

popbooksonline.com/haunted-jewels

*Scanning QR codes requires a web-enabled smart device with a QR code reader app and a camera.

TABLE OF CONTENTS

CHAPTER 1
Ghostly Gems 4

CHAPTER 2
Everyone Loves a Curse 8

CHAPTER 3
Stolen Treasure 16

CHAPTER 4
The Ring 22

Making Connections 30
Glossary 31
Index 32
Online Resources 32

CHAPTER 1

GHOSTLY GEMS

Some gems are difficult to come by. Certain kinds of natural crystals are especially rare and beautiful. They formed billions of years ago deep in Earth's crust. Heat and weight combined to make diamonds, emeralds, and other

WATCH A VIDEO HERE!

Jewelry is often handed down through families.

kinds of precious jewels. Natural events like earthquakes push them to the surface. People dig in the earth to look for them.

Since jewels are so rare, they are very expensive. It is a sign of great wealth when people wear jewelry with precious gems. Families have fought over the beautiful pieces throughout history.

Some people use jewelry to express themselves through style.

Royals used to be the only people who could afford expensive jewelry.

Besides money, people steal or start wars to get their hands on famous jewelry. It's no wonder some pieces become cursed and haunted.

Haunted jewelry is beautiful and dangerous. For some people, that makes the jewelry even more exciting and special.

CHAPTER 2
EVERYONE LOVES A CURSE

The Hope Diamond necklace is a well-known piece of haunted jewelry. It's been included in popular songs and had a major part in the famous film *Titanic*.

LEARN MORE HERE!

The heart-shaped necklace used in the Titanic *movie was called the Heart of the Ocean.*

But even without the lights of Hollywood upon it, the Hope Diamond's real story is quite exciting.

The amazing blue diamond was discovered in India. The gem was 112 **carats**. That is very big! French royalty bought it in 1668. They cut it down to 45.5 carats. The diamond stayed with the crown for a hundred years until the king and queen were killed during the French Revolution. All the royal riches were stolen. The blue diamond disappeared.

 **DID YOU KNOW?** France was in such chaos that no one noticed the thieves sneak off with the crown's jewels.

It reappeared in London 20 years later. Once again, the stone was cut smaller. In 1839, it received its name. The Hope family bought it. They fought over it for **generations**! The Hopes eventually had to sell it to cover **gambling** debt.

THE FRENCH REVOLUTION

The French Revolution lasted from 1789 to 1799. The poor and working-class people of France destroyed and rebuilt their government. They had grown tired of watching their leaders run the country irresponsibly. People were starving to death while King Louis the Sixteenth and Queen Marie-Antoinette were spending the country's money on clothes and parties. So, the people took to the streets and killed all the leaders they thought were hurting the country.

The now famous jeweler Pierre Cartier brought the diamond to the United States. He put the diamond into the necklace it is in today.

Cartier spread stories that the Hope Diamond was cursed. He said the man who dug it up was ripped apart by dogs. Cartier bragged about it belonging to King Louis the Sixteenth and Queen Marie-Antoinette before their tragic deaths. Curses were trending in books and entertainment during the early 1900s. Cartier knew that an eerie story would help him sell the gem for more money.

Before TV commercials, store displays drew many customers to make large jewelry purchases.

Sure enough, the story captured **heiress** Evalyn McLean's attention. To be safe, she got the Hope Diamond blessed before she brought it home. Evalyn loved to brag about the diamond and its curse when she wore it at parties. Sometimes she let her dog wear the necklace as

Evalyn also owned another famous jewel called the Star of the East.

14

a collar. Unfortunately for Evalyn, she started to experience bad luck. Her husband ran away with another woman, and one of her young sons was hit by a car.

She kept the jewel even after her daughter died tragically. Evalyn was wearing it when she died. The Hope Diamond was meant to stay in the family. But Evalyn owed so much money after her death, it had to be sold. The necklace ended up on display in the Smithsonian Museum in Washington, DC.

CHAPTER 3

STOLEN TREASURE

Many pieces of ancient jewelry end up in museums. They tell stories about the people who made them thousands of years ago. In the case of the **Lydian Hoard**, the jewelry was **looted** from a princess's tomb in Turkey 2,000 years after she died.

LEARN MORE HERE!

There are 363 pieces of treasure in the Lydian Hoard.

The Lydian Hoard is a collection of gold and silver objects discovered by thieves in 1966. The most famous piece is the golden hippocamp **pendant**. A hippocamp is a make-believe creature that is half horse and half fish. The curse of this treasure hit quickly according to the villagers who knew the thieves.

PARTS OF A HIPPOCAMPUS

The hippocampus is a make-believe creature. It was the size of a horse and lived in deep parts of the ocean. Hippocampus swam in groups. Stories of these creatures described them as kind and loyal. They were known to rescue sailors who were in trouble.

After selling the collection to **smugglers**, the thieves' bad luck began. They were captured by police. But things got worse. One of the robbers was murdered. Some lost their children to horrible accidents. Another robber was injured and couldn't walk again. The robber who lived the longest went mad.

 If someone finds ancient treasure, the person usually has to give it to the government of whatever land it was found on.

People fought over where the treasure would end up. It was sold illegally to the New York City's Metropolitan Museum of Art. Turkey demanded it be returned to them. After a battle in court, the Lydian Hoard was given back to its home country.

Some think that when a treasure is taken from where it belongs, negative energy attaches to it. This brings bad luck to those handling it. Even once it was home, the Lydian Hoard didn't rest. Part of it was stolen again! The Uşak Museum director switched the golden hippocamp with a fake. He was going to sell it to pay off his **gambling** debts. He blamed his financial problems on the curse.

The hoard is still on display in Turkey. Many are careful about how close they get to it in case it truly is cursed!

The Metropolitan Museum of Art has a few of its own ghosts running through the halls.

CHAPTER 4

THE RING

In England, it's not strange to come across ancient gold coins or swords when digging in the dirt. Many groups of people moved around the area throughout history. A farmer found the famous Ring

COMPLETE AN ACTIVITY HERE!

In 2009 a treasure hoard worth millions of dollars was discovered in a farmer's field.

of Silvianus in 1785 while working in his field. He sold it to the Chute family, who collected old treasures.

Ruins are common in English countrysides.

The Chutes studied it and learned it dated back nearly 2,000 years to the Roman Empire. On the ring was a picture of the goddess Venus and the words "Senicianus live well in god" written in

Latin. Some of the words were spelled incorrectly. Sanicianus was thought to have owned the ring. The Chute family kept the ring for **generations**.

An illustration of the infamous Ring of Silvianus.

An **archaeologist** named Sir Mortimer Wheeler made a surprising discovery about the ring 200 years later.

People carved love spells into stone tablets too.

DID YOU KNOW? Cursed tablets were popular during Silvianus's time. They are called *defixios*.

The field the ring was found in was near the ruins of a **Celtic** temple for the god Noden. Also found nearby was a stone tablet with a curse written out on it. It said a gold ring belonging to Silvianus had been stolen by a man named Senicianus. It promised the god Noden half the ring's worth if good fortune never befell Senicianus again.

Wheeler didn't know what to make of the cursed tablet and ring, so he asked a friend for help. His friend was J.R.R. Tolkien. The two decided that Senicianus might have put his name on the ring soon after he stole it. That is why it was misspelled; it was a rushed job. Perhaps he wanted to make it seem like the ring was his if he was ever caught.

No one truly knows what happened to Senicianus after he stole the ring. He may have lived a hard life and died alone. But the ring kept people interested for thousands of years. Its curse inspired Tolkien. He went on to write some of the most famous fantasy books ever about a cursed ring. *The Hobbit* and *The Lord of the Rings* are about the pain and adventure cursed jewelry can create.

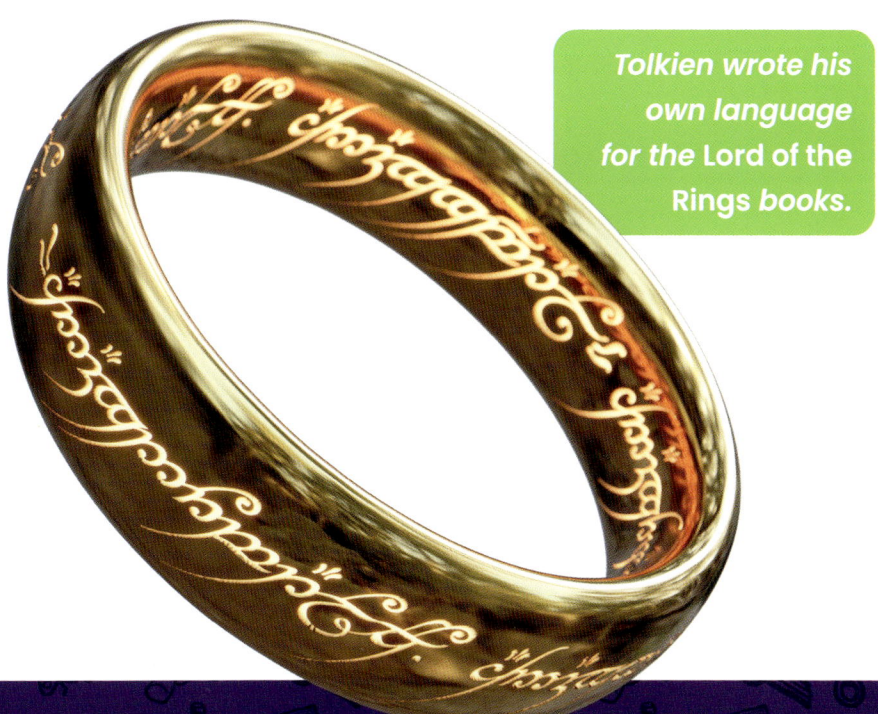

Tolkien wrote his own language for the Lord of the Rings **books.**

MAKING CONNECTIONS

TEXT-TO-SELF

Would you wear a piece of cursed jewelry? If so, which one? If not, what is stopping you?

TEXT-TO-TEXT

Have you read any other books about cursed objects? What did they have in common with the jewelry in this book?

TEXT-TO-WORLD

Why do you think people are so interested in jewelry? What has owning expensive jewelry meant throughout history?

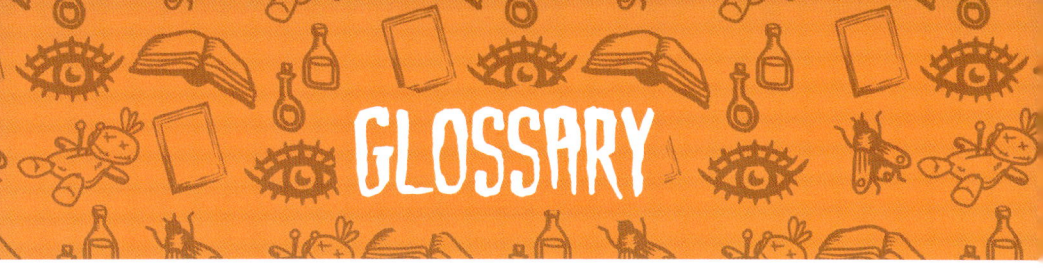

GLOSSARY

archaeologist — a scientist who studies materials of past human life.

carat — a unit for measuring precious stones.

Celt — a person who lived 2,000 years ago in many countries of western Europe.

gamble — to bet money on games such as cards or slot machines.

generation — family members who are usually about the same age.

heir — a person who receives great wealth.

hoard — a collection of things often stored or hidden away.

loot — to steal.

pendant — a part of a necklace that hangs freely.

smuggle — to bring in or send out something secretly and illegally.

INDEX

Chute family, 23–25

curse, 12, 17, 21, 27, 29

England, 22

French Revolution, 10–11

hippocamp, 17–18, 21

McLean, Evelyn, 14–15

money, 6–7, 11–12, 15

Roman Empire, 24

Titanic, 8

Tolkien, J.R.R., 28–29

Turkey, 16, 20

Wheeler, Mortimer, 26, 28

ONLINE RESOURCES
popbooksonline.com

Scan this code* and others like it while you read, or visit the website below to make this book pop!

popbooksonline.com/haunted-jewels

*Scanning QR codes requires a web-enabled smart device with a QR code reader app and a camera.